TODDLERS
Stories for Bedtime

Illustrated by Eric Kincaid

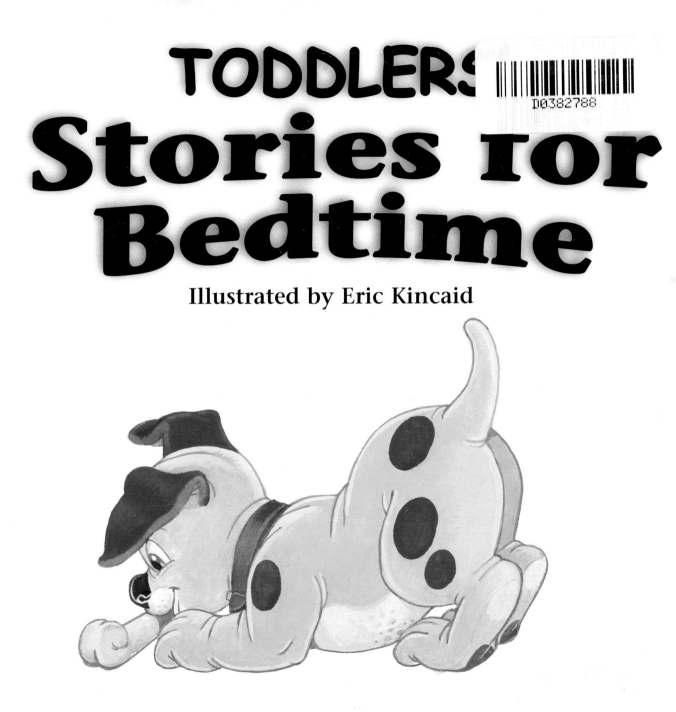

Contents

Scamp is Naughty!   6

Daisy is Lost   24

Carrots for Rosie   42

Charlie's New Nest   60

Scamp is Naughty!

Scamp the puppy is looking for his bone. He cannot remember where he left it. Scamp looks under the table.

Scamp is naughty!
He pulls the tablecloth off
the table. He hasn't found
his bone, either.

Scamp looks in the garden instead. He is naughty! He starts to dig a hole. Now his paws are muddy. He still hasn't found his bone.

Scamp goes back indoors.
He looks on the sofa.
He is naughty! He makes
the cushions muddy. He still
hasn't found his bone.

Scamp goes into the kitchen. He is naughty! He spills the water in his bowl. He still hasn't found his bone.

Scamp looks in the bedroom. He is naughty! He pulls the pillows off the bed. He still hasn't found his bone.

Scamp stops to have a rest.
Where is his bone?
He tries to remember...
Then at last he does!

Scamp goes back into
the kitchen. He looks under
the blanket in his basket.

There is Scamp's bone! He wags his tail. Maybe Scamp won't be naughty anymore!

Daisy is Lost

Daisy the duck is swimming on the river. The sun is shining and Daisy is very happy. She loves to swim!

Daisy takes a deep breath and dives deep under the water. She says hello to all the fish she sees.

Then Daisy sees her
friend, Frog.
"Hello, Frog!" calls Daisy.
"Let's play!"

Daisy and Frog play in the water. They have great fun swimming races. Soon it is time to go home. Frog waves goodbye.

Daisy looks around.
She doesn't know where
she is. She is afraid.

Daisy climbs onto the
river bank.
"Oh, no," she says to
herself. "I am lost."

Daisy's brothers are worried about her. She should have been home a long time ago. They decide to go and look for her.

Daisy can hear her brothers calling her.
"Daisy! Quack! Quack!
Where are you?"

At last Daisy's brothers find her. Daisy is very happy to see them. She is not lost anymore.

Carrots for Rosie

Rosie the rabbit is always hungry. She is fed up with eating grass. She wants something different to eat.

Rosie sees a caterpillar
on the ground.
She twitches her nose.
"I cannot eat a caterpillar,"
says Rosie.

Then Rosie sees a path.
She decides to follow it.
"I might find something nice
to eat on the way," says
Rosie.

Rosie comes to a barn.
There is a hole in the side.
"I wonder what is in here?"
says Rosie.
She goes in to have a look.

Rosie finds a big box
filled with juicy apples.
She starts to eat one.
"I love eating apples!"
says Rosie.

Then Rosie finds some
crunchy carrots.
"I love eating carrots!"
says Rosie.

Rosie is still hungry.
She sees some crisp, juicy
lettuces. She eats those
too. Rosie eats and eats
and eats!

Rosie is full up. She does not feel well. Her tummy is aching. She wishes she hadn't eaten so much. Rosie goes home to her mother.

"I've eaten too much and now I have a tummy ache," says Rosie to her mother. "Then you shouldn't have been so greedy!" says Mother Rabbit.

Charlie's New Nest

Charlie is a little, yellow chick. He has six brothers and sisters. They all live in a nest. There isn't much room. Sometimes Charlie gets squashed!

In fact, there are so many chicks in the nest, Charlie cannot go to sleep.
"I wish there was more room in this little nest," says Charlie.

The other chicks are too busy making room for themselves. They do not notice when Charlie falls out of the nest. He is not very happy!

"I must find a new nest," says Charlie. "I will look around the farmyard." Charlie finds an old hat.

Charlie jumps inside the hat.
"This will make a lovely nest,
just for me!" he says.
Now Charlie must make the
hat snug and warm.

Charlie finds a feather.
He takes it back to the hat.
"This will make my nest
lovely and warm," he says.

Next Charlie finds some
soft, fluffy dandelions.
He takes them back to the
hat, one by one.
"These will make my nest
soft to sleep in,"
says Charlie.

At last the hat is ready.
"I have a warm, soft nest of
my very own," says Charlie.
"There is plenty of room to
sleep in now."

Charlie has worked
hard to get his nest ready.
He is very tired. Soon he is
snug, warm - and fast
asleep!